W9-AZX-757

VIKING KESTREL
Viking Penguin Inc., 40 West 23rd Street
New York, New York 10010, U.S.A.
Penguin Books Canada Limited, 2801 John Street
Markham, Ontario, Canada L3R 1B4

First published in 1989 by Viking Penguin Inc.
Published simultaneously in Canada
Set in Sabon.
Printed and bound in Italy
Created and Produced by Sadie Fields Productions Ltd,
8, Pembridge Studios, 27A Pembridge Villas, London W11 3EP

1 2 3 4 5 93 92 91 90 89

I'm Brave!

Karen Erickson and Maureen Roffey

Viking Kestrel

Oh, no! I fell down.

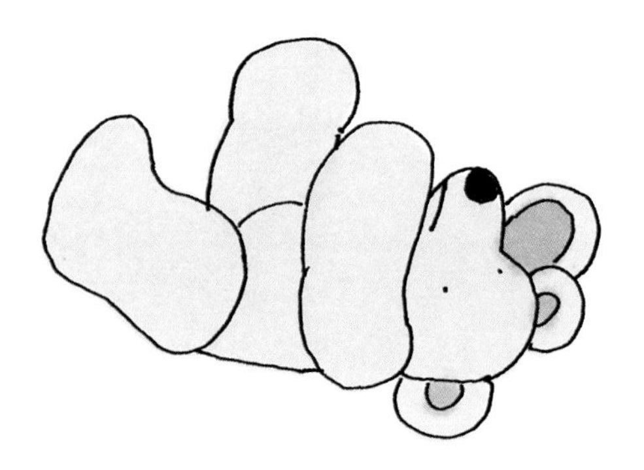

My arm aches. My knee burns.

I feel terrible.
I want to scream and shout.

I wish I'd never learned to run.

I want Daddy to hug me and
make the hurt go away.

But Daddy says everyone
hurts themselves sometimes.

He says it's okay to cry.
But after you stop, be brave.

The medicine might sting,
but I will soon feel better.

All right, I won't cry anymore.

I'll scrunch up my face,
close my eyes and
take deep breaths.

Look. It works.

I can be brave.
I can do it.
I did it.